£5.70

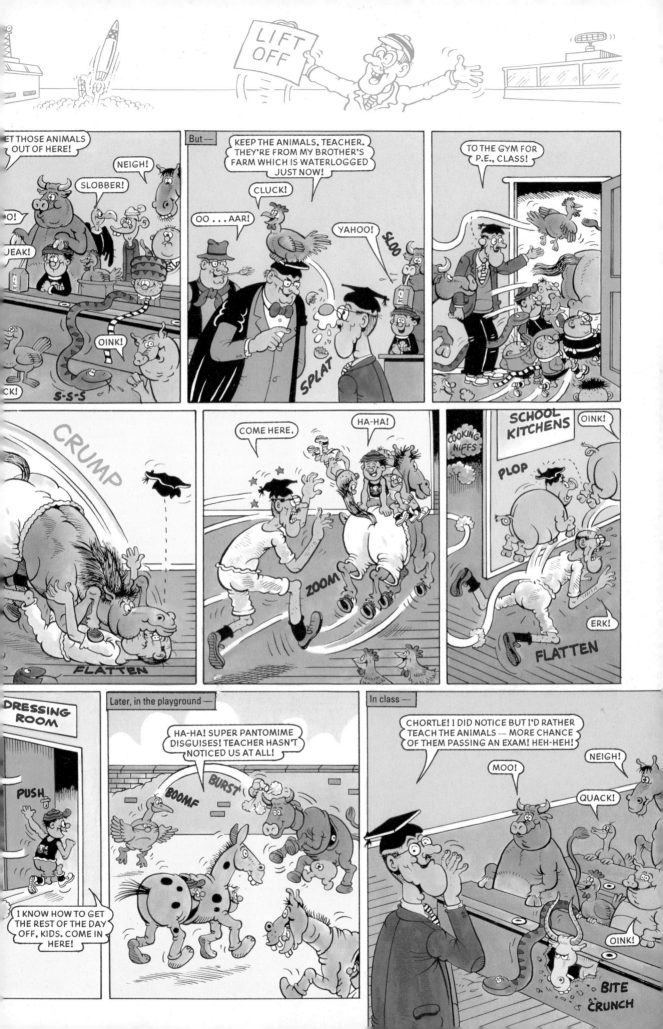

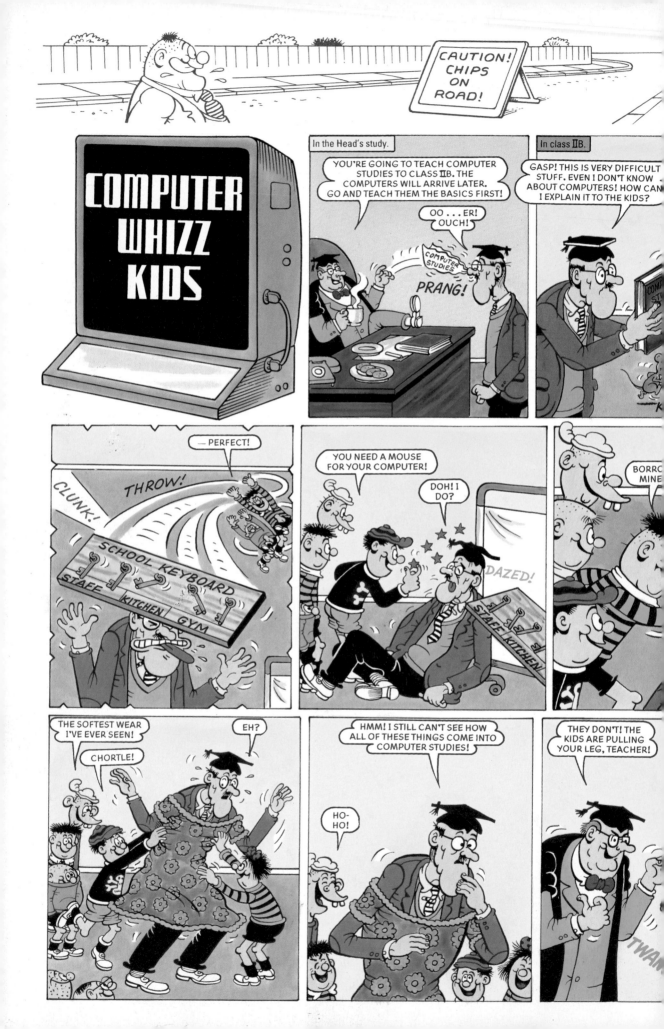

# SITUATIONS VACANT

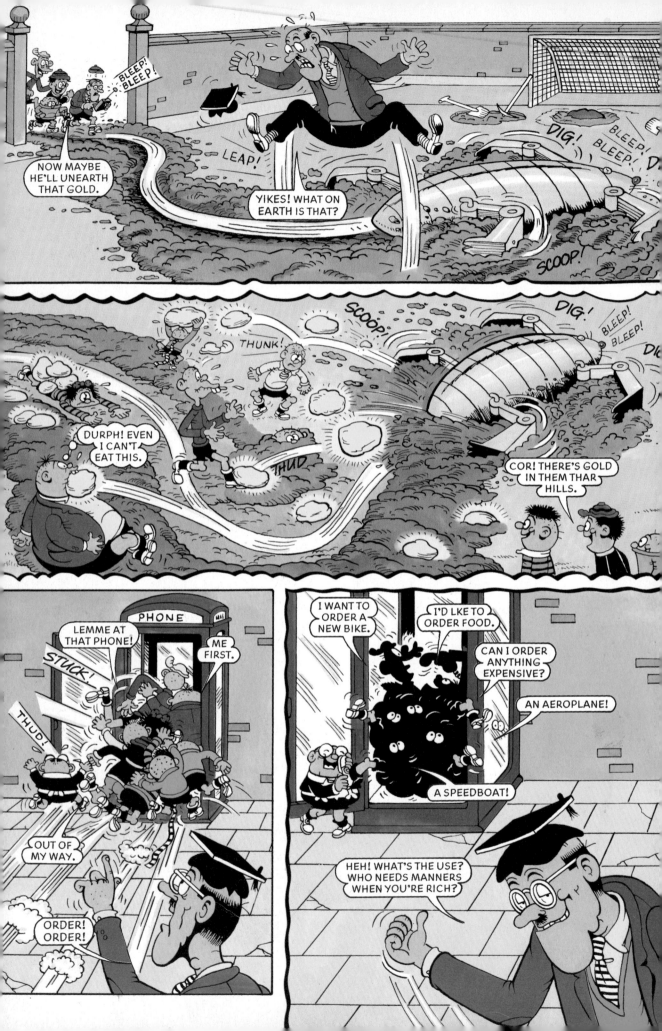

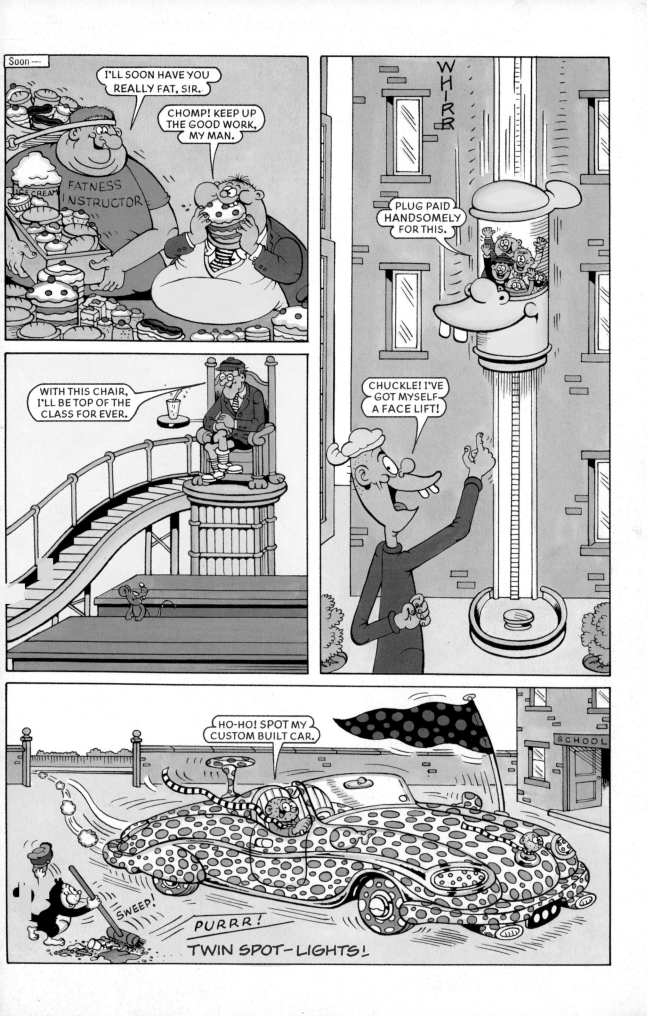

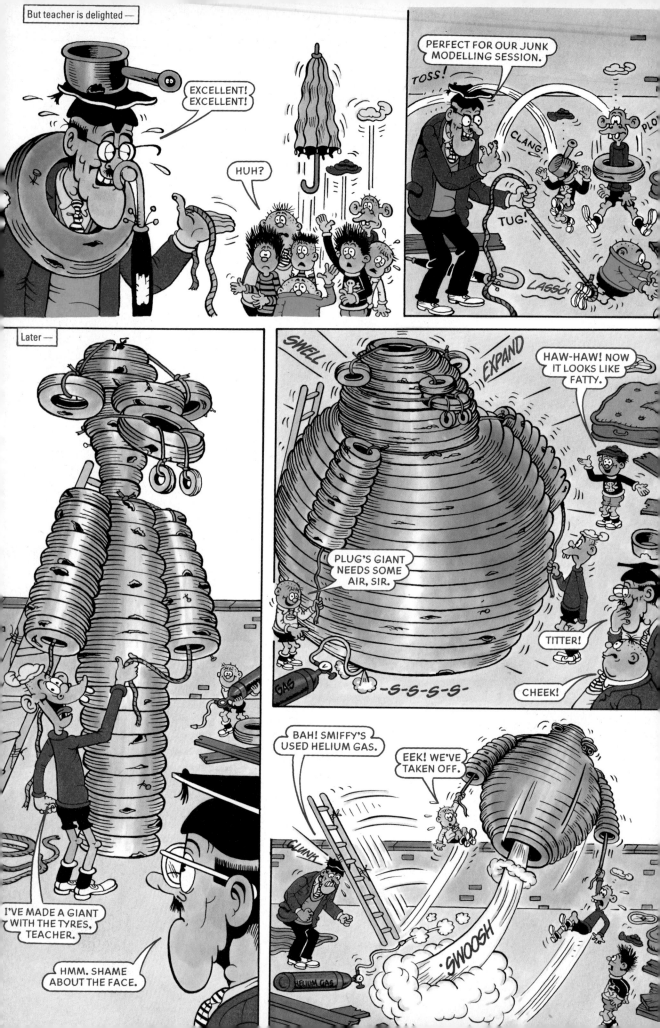

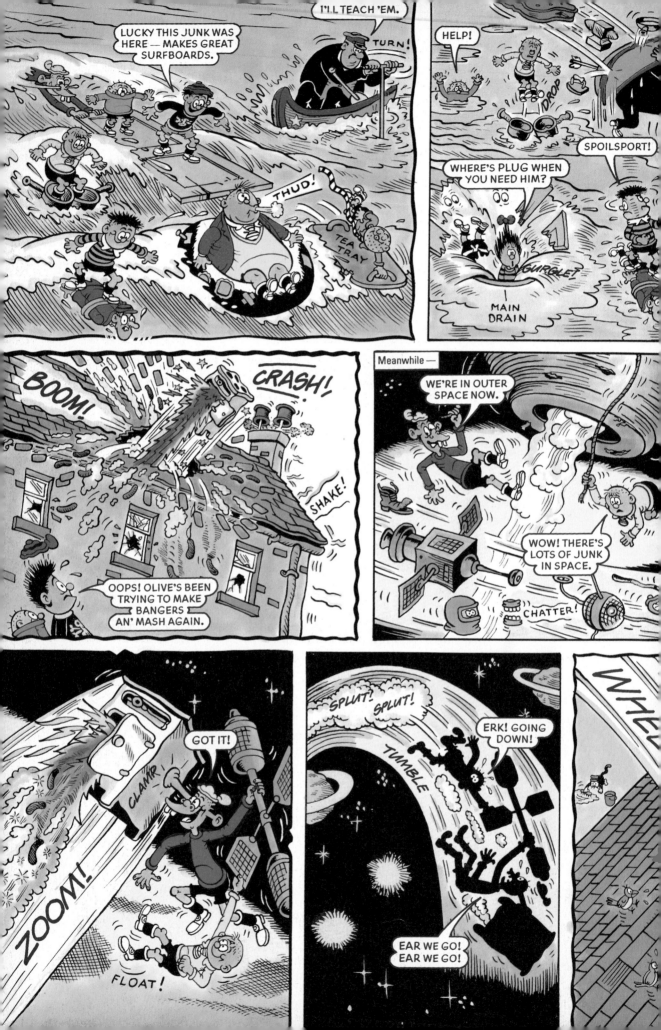

# SITUATIONS VACANT

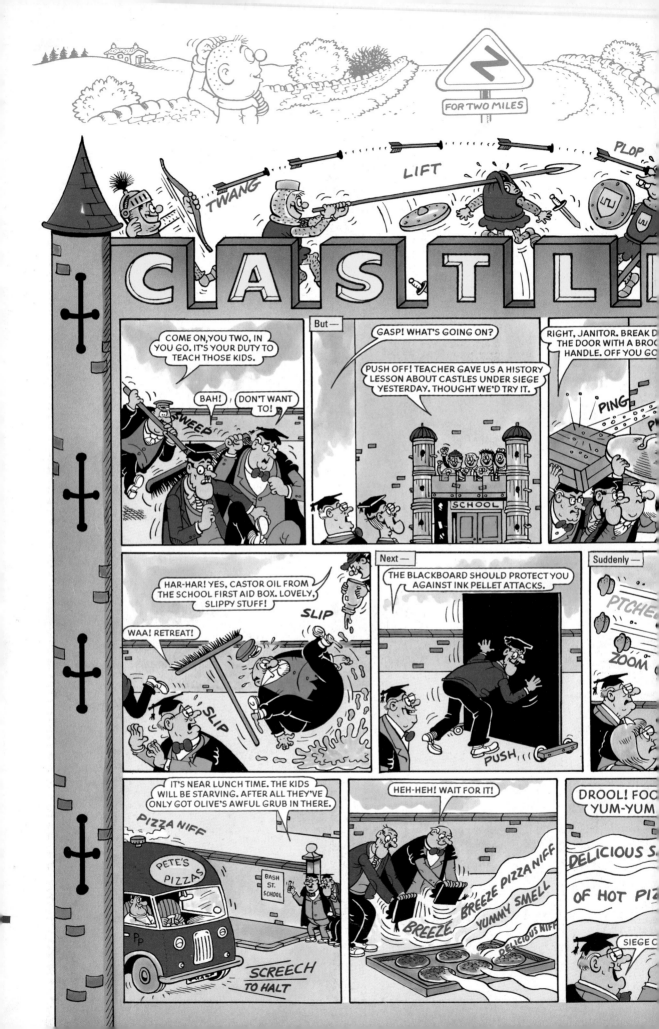

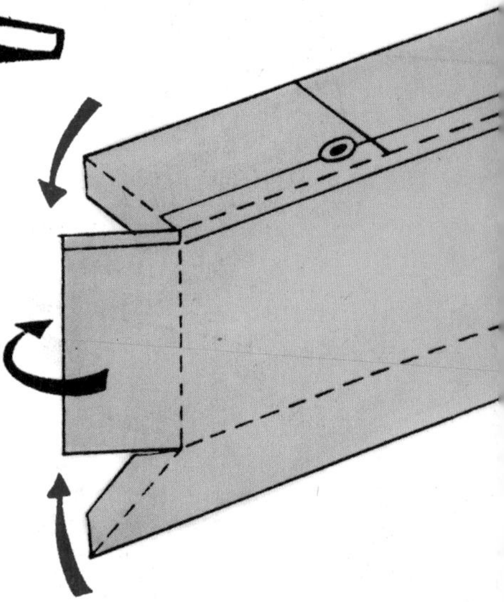

# CUT IT OUT!

**How's your aim with an elastic band? Here's a tester for you and your pals, for a rainy day.**

Copy the desks and figures shown on the next few pages on to card (or, if you have access to a photocopier, even better to use that!) and construct your classroom, as shown in the diagrams. Stick them all down on a baseboard, and you're all set for a game!

Award points for each figure, and see how many you can hit, from two metres away! (Bonus points for hitting Teacher, Headmaster or Janitor!)

FOLD HERE

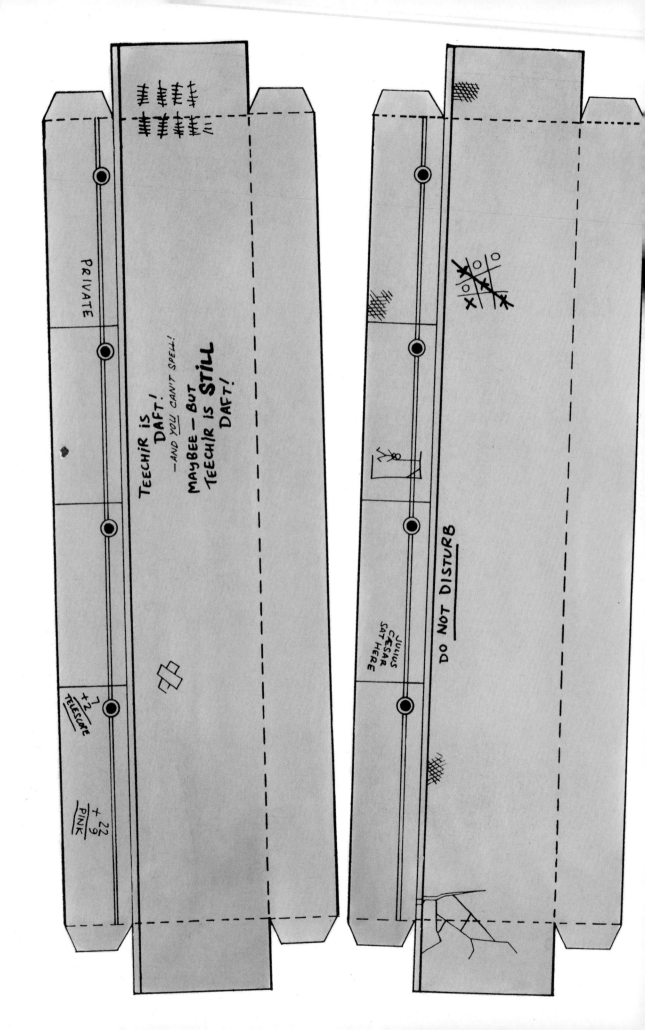

JANITOR

FOLD HERE

FOLD HERE

FOLD HERE

FOLD HERE

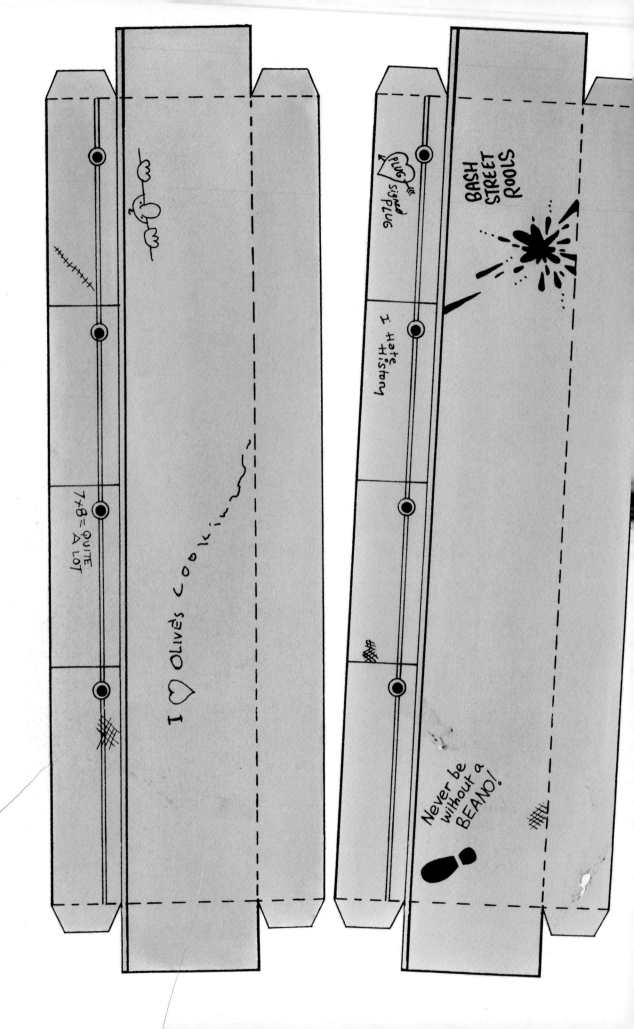

FOLD HERE

FOLD HERE

FOLD HERE

FOLD HERE

FOLD HERE

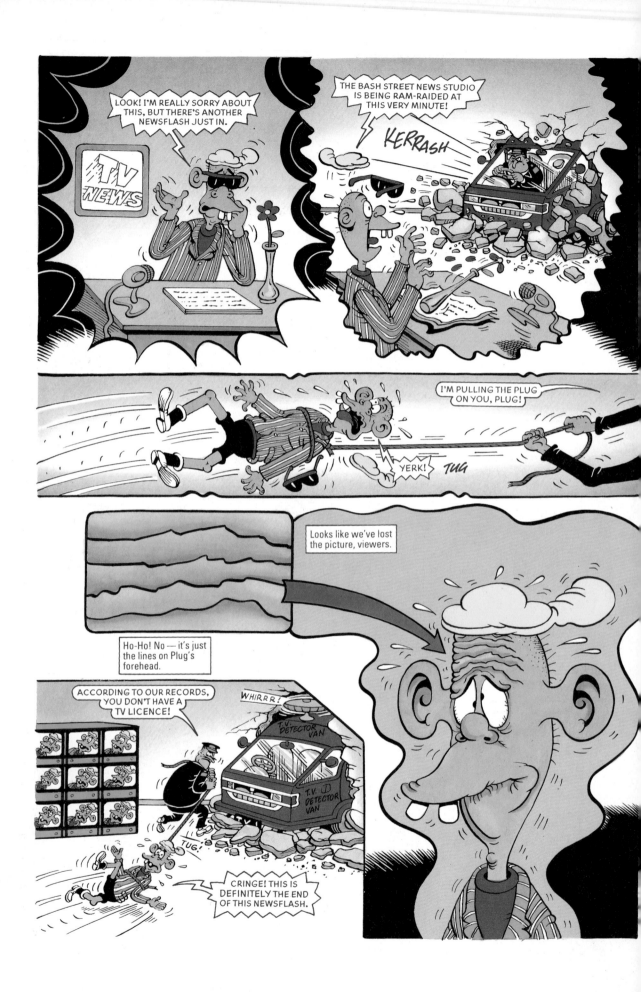

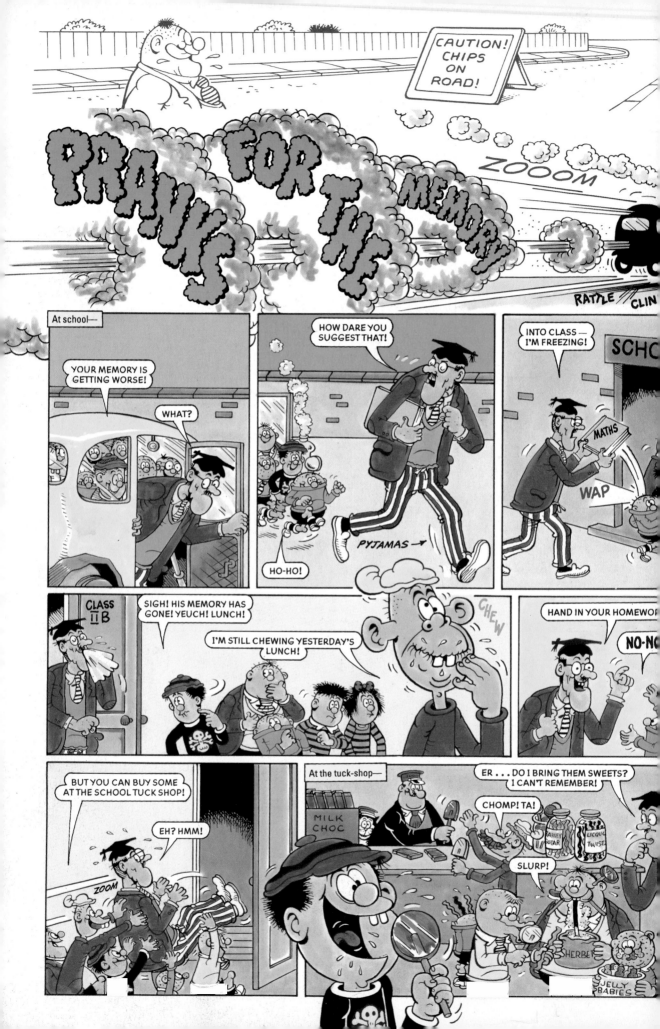